The Christmas Fox

AND OTHER WINTER POEMS BY JOHN BUSH

PICTURES BY Peter Weevers

Dial Books for Young Readers | New York

Otto Skates

In the white of winter, on a still, clear day,
Otto is giving a skating display;
Gracefully sliding and gliding with ease
With a swish of his skates and a bend of his knees.

With hand on one hip, tail stretched out straight,
Perfectly poised to balance his weight;
His father was Woodland champion, they say,
And *he* taught Otto to skate that way.

Silently, smoothly, he circles and whirls
Through figures of eight and breathtaking twirls,
With never a slip or the slightest mistake.
Did you ever think that an otter could skate?

First published in the United States 1989 by
Dial Books for Young Readers
A Division of Penguin Books USA Inc.
2 Park Avenue
New York, New York 10016
Published in Great Britain by Hutchinson Children's Books Ltd
Text copyright © 1988 by John Bush
Illustrations copyright © 1988 by Peter Weevers
Printed in Italy
First Edition
D
1 3 5 7 9 10 8 6 4 2

Library of Congress Cataloging in Publication Data
Bush, John.
The Christmas Fox and other winter poems.
Summary: A collection of poems about the winter
activities of a variety of animals.
1. Winter—Juvenile poetry. 2. Animals—Juvenile
poetry. 3. Children's poetry, English. [1. Winter—
Poetry. 2. Animals—Poetry. 3. English poetry.]
I. Weevers, Peter, ill. II. Title.
PR6052.U766C47   1989   821'.914   89-1122
ISBN 0-8037-0723-1

The art consists of watercolor paintings,
which are camera-separated and reproduced in full color.

Milly Sits and Knits

With patient fingers, so nimble and quick,
Milly Mouse knits, clickety click;
Glasses perched on the end of her nose
As she carefully counts the rows.

Knit Milly Mouse as you sit and rock,
And your needles click and tick like a clock;
Knit by the candlelight yellow and pale,
But do take care not to rock on your tail!

The Goose of Toulouse

Have you heard the news? Have you heard the
   news?
She's here! The fashionable Goose of Toulouse!
With an elegant boa of downy, white feathers
And red, tassled shawl to keep out the weather.

Her hat is tied down with silk ribbons, just so,
And adorned with a sprig of fresh mistletoe.
She looks a fine sight, you must confess.
The French are known for the way they dress.

As she stands on the bank of the iced-over river,
The thought of a swim, sets her a-shiver.
"Mon Dieu!" she honks. "If you ask my views,
Winter is never this cold in Toulouse."

Blaireau Badger

This snow!" snorts Blaireau, "such tiresome stuff.
Snow! Snow! Snow! I've had enough!
I no sooner clear it from my door,
When it comes down, harder than before.

"Time was once I found this fun,
When these paws were strong and young.
As a cub, I *liked* the cold.
But now I'm getting far too old.

"And every winter I need more clothes,
To keep the chill out of my toes.
Still, there's a time for everything,
And after winter comes – the spring."

Emilina Hedgehog

In her cozy little room, snuggled up in bed,
Emilina Hedgehog pulls the covers to her head.
Peeking out by candlelight, she reads her favorite
    story,
Of how her great-grandfather won fortune, fame,
    and glory.

Wilberforce was his name; a sailor bold was he,
Who discovered hedgehog continents across the
    Woodland Sea.
And there's a part that always brings a tear to
    Emmie's eyes,
When Wilberforce is knighted and the queen says,
    "Sir, arise."

But proud of her great-grandfather as Emilina is,
She's rather glad that *her* life is more quiet and
    safe than his.
There's no place that she'd rather be, of that she is
    quite sure,
Than snuggled in her winter bed – cozy and secure.

The Christmas Fox

O Father Christmas! You don't look the same
As the jolly, round fellow who goes by that name.
Where's your white beard? Your face is so sly.
There's a point to your ears and a glint in your eye.

And what of your sack? A turkey's no toy!
Hardly the gift for a girl or a boy.
No black boots. No snowy locks.
You're *not* Father Christmas, you're O'Farley the
  Fox!

But O'Farley just smiles as on through the snow
He toils and trudges, ever so slow.
His sack bows his back and the strain has him
  hobbling,
But he smiles for he knows just who'll do the
  gobbling.

Will and Mrs. Finch

At last the falling snow has stopped, so Mrs. Finch
and Will
Have popped outside to breathe the air and now are
sitting still.
"I thought that snow would never end," Will twitters
to his wife,
"Never seen it snow like that, never in my life."

"Chilly out here, isn't it?" says Mrs. Finch to Will.
"These new scarves I knitted us, they'll keep away
the chill."
"Yes, indeed," Will replies, "and your hat, I see,
Suits you very well.my dear; it matches perfectly."

"Why, thank you, Will!" chirps Mrs. Finch, giving him
a kiss.
"I think we make a handsome pair perched out here,
like this."
"That we do," Will agrees, "and I'll tell you true;
None in all the wide Woodland is prettier than you."

The North Country Stoat

O creatures beware the North Country Stoat,
Who prowls about in his ermine coat.
O sharp are his teeth and long are his claws,
Close up your windows and lock up your doors.

And see, the sleek Stoat is on somebody's track.
O whoever you are, hurry home, don't look back!
For the North Country Stoat follows behind you
And you know what will happen if he should find
   you.

O hurry! O hurry! Whoever you are,
I do hope your home is safe and not far.
For the North Country Stoat follows behind you
*And you know what will happen if he should find
   you!*

A Dormouse's House

There's nothing that a dormouse loves quite so
  much as sleeping,
That's why a dormouse never does quite enough
  housekeeping.
No sooner does a dormouse start, when suddenly
  he's yawning
And thinking that it all can wait until another
  morning.

There's a tatter in the curtain that hangs across
  the door,
And curly leaves the wind's blown in are lying on
  the floor.
The furniture needs dusting, there're cobwebs on
  the ceiling,
But just the thought of all that work starts a
  drowsy feeling.

Ask any Woodland creature, they'll tell you that it's
  true:
In every dormouse house you'll find there's lots and
  lots to do.
A little mending here and there, some dusting or
  some sweeping,
For there's nothing that a dormouse loves quite so
  much as sleeping.

Roy Robin

Roy Robin, Roy Robin, where are you going?
What will you do if it starts snowing?
It's much too cold to be flying about.
Do go home! O don't stay out!"

"But I'm not cold, not whatsoever –
Never too cold, if you dress for the weather.
I have my cap with its little bell,
And I'm wrapped in a nice warm scarf, as well."

"You do look chirpy, and your eyes are bright;
They twinkle like ice as it catches the light.
But pray do tell me, when it snows,
Doesn't the cold ever get to your toes?"

If Mooses Were Gooses

O dear! O dear! O deary me!
How I wish a moose could ski!
The trouble when it snows and snows is
We get stuck up to our noses.

"And O the effort to get out!
The time it takes to move about!
You just can't find a thing to chew.
O *what* is a poor moose to do!

"I wish, O how I wish we mooses
Could fly above the ground like gooses,
Because at times like this the truth is,
Wings and feathers have their uses."

Crawford the Crow

"Winter is coming!" cries Crawford the Crow.
"There's a chill in the air, a chill I well know.
The last leaves are falling, the whiteness will come,
'Twill be a long time till we feel the warm sun.

"Soon hill and valley will sleep under snow.
And the rough, raw, rushing winds will blow.
For an undertaker such as I,
'Tis a cruel, cold time to collect bones by.

"And these poor knees freeze, and these wings won't
      flap,
And you can't get a drink for the ice on a tap.
Oh, no! No! No! If the choice were mine
I'd wish for summer, all the time!"